THE ADVENTURE CLUB

RED PANDA RESCUE

JESS BUTTERWORTH

Orion

ORION CHILDREN'S BOOKS

First published in Great Britain in 2021 by Orion Children's Books

1 3 5 7 9 10 8 6 4 2

A CIP catalogue record for this book
is available from the British Library.

ISBN 978 1 510 10796 0

Printed and bound in Great Britain by
Clays Ltd, Elcograf, S.p.A.

The paper and board used in this book
are made from wood from responsible sources.

MIX
Paper from
responsible sources
FSC
www.fsc.org   FSC® C104740

Orion Children's Books
An imprint of
Hachette Children's Group
Part of Hodder and Stoughton
Carmelite House
50 Victoria Embankment
London EC4Y 0DZ

An Hachette UK Company
www.hachette.co.uk

www.hachettechildrens.co.uk

To Matilda, Leo, and every young adventurer

This adventure notebook belongs to Tilly. (That's me.)
I'm eight years old. In it, I'm going to write down all
my adventures. I just hope I get to go on some ...

School, Monday, 11am

There are three weeks left of school until the spring holidays and everyone is excited.

Except me.

This morning, **EVERYONE** was talking about their big plans while we waited for Ms Perry.

'I'm going on a narrowboat holiday this year!' said Charlotte.

'I'm going surfing in Cornwall!' said Mo, miming being on a surfboard.

'I'm going camping!' said Oliver.

I sighed and looked at the clock, counting down the minutes until the lunch break. Mum, Dad and I have just moved across the country for Mum's new job as an engineer. And since Mum has to work, and Dad is away being a boat captain, I'll be stuck with a babysitter.

But really, it's going to be ...

And ...

Which gives me an idea for this notebook! I'm not going to sit around and wait for adventures any more ... I'm going to create my own! And my first task is to make some friends.

The First Adventure

> **Objective:** Make new friends.
>
> **Obstacles:** Everyone here already has friends. I don't know anyone yet. Sometimes, it takes me a while to feel comfortable around new people.

School, Monday, lunch

The **BEST** thing has just happened. I know my handwriting is messy but it's because I'm writing quickly 'cos I simply **HAVE** to tell you right away.

It was almost the end of morning lessons and I was yawning in class when Ms Perry said, '... which brings me to my exciting announcement.'

Everyone stopped whispering and paid attention.

'Our school has been chosen to participate in the Adventure Club. The Adventure Club is a group of scientists and nature experts who take kids on trips around the world to learn about endangered animals from people that live alongside them. And this spring, one of our students will get the chance to go to Nepal to monitor red pandas!'

'What does monitor mean?' asked Mo.

'To monitor something means to observe it,' replied Ms Perry. 'The chosen student will get to observe red pandas in the wild to check how they are doing and write it down.'

I gasped. I loved animals. And I was **ALREADY** writing about my adventures **RIGHT HERE** in my notebook. This was everything I wanted my holidays to be!

The room buzzed with excitement.

'What's a red panda?' asked Deepa. 'Is it like a panda bear?'

'Where's Nepal?' asked Claire. 'How long would

we be there?'

'How many schools were chosen?' asked Tom.

'Just three schools,' said Ms Perry. 'One student from each school will go. Nepal is in Asia and the trip is seven days long – plus two days of travelling. And what was the other question? No, red pandas are not like giant pandas.'

I grinned and straightened my back. This was **PERFECT**! If I went to Nepal, everyone would want to be my friend and hear about my adventures! I **HAD** to find a way to go. The lunch bell rang and everyone started shuffling in their seats.

'If you want to apply,' Ms Perry went on, 'make sure you take a copy of the newsletter with more details and this form for your parents to sign.' Ms Perry pointed to a stack of papers on her desk.

'And there will be an assembly about the club

next week in the evening for your parents to attend.'

Everyone leapt up from their chairs, chattering about the Adventure Club.

Can you believe it?! I'm eating my lunch at super-speed now and I'm going to head straight to the library before the next lesson to find out everything I can about red pandas and Nepal.

The library, Monday, just after lunch
This day keeps getting better and better! I'm in the library and a few minutes ago I was searching the shelves for books about red pandas when another **AMAZING** thing happened. I already feel like I'm having adventures and I haven't even left school!

There were books on giant panda bears and grizzly bears but no red panda books. Another challenge!

I wrote it down in my book.

The Second Adventure

Objective: Learn about red pandas.

Obstacles: Finding the right book!

I marched up to the librarian, Ms May.

'Excuse me please, Ms May,' I said. 'Do you have any books about red pandas? It's **VERY** important.'

Ms May smiled. 'Let me see.'

After a minute she returned holding a hardback called *Animals of the Mountains*. She flicked through the pages.

'This book talks about all different kinds of animals that live in the mountains, including red pandas.'

I beamed at her. 'Thank you.'

'Are you finding out about red pandas too?' asked a familiar voice from behind me.

I turned around. It was Charlotte from my class. Her long, red hair was tied up with a green hairband that matched her eyes.

I nodded and chewed my lip, wondering if she wanted to read together.

'You can look at this book with me?' I decided to suggest. 'I think it's the **ONLY** one about red pandas.'

'Brilliant!' said Charlotte.

We sat down together at a table and skimmed past pages of eagles, monkeys and snow leopards. I paused at the pictures of tigers. I **LOVED** tigers, maybe I'd get to see one! But the book said there were only 230 in the whole of Nepal so I probably wouldn't. Finally, we reached the red panda pages.

'Oh my gosh, they're so cute!' said Charlotte.

I had imagined a red panda
would look like this:

But really, it looks like this:

I stared at the image. A fluffy face with white
markings and big eyes stared back. It had a bushy

red tail with white rings all down it.

More than anything, I wanted to see one for real.
Charlotte and I wrote a list of red
panda facts.

Red Pandas ...
- Are not actually related to giant pandas
- Make a twittering sound
- Eat mainly bamboo leaves and shoots
- Are good at camouflaging in fir trees
- Live in a high, mountain forest habitat, mostly
in trees
- Are found in the Eastern Himalayas in Nepal,
Tibet, China, Bhutan, India and Myanmar

'I hope one of us gets to join the Adventure
Club,' said Charlotte, when we'd finished.

'Me too,' I replied, smiling.

Then Charlotte left, and I got out my notebook to update it before class. I cut and glued the paper with the red panda facts into my notebook. I didn't want to lose them!

So that's the second exciting thing that happened today ... I made my first friend at this new school!

Home, Monday, in bed

I think I've almost convinced Mum to let me apply for the Adventure Club.

When I got home after school, I strode determinedly into the kitchen.

I handed Mum the school newsletter and told her it was **EXTREMELY** important she read it right now.

I watched her anxiously. She frowned.

'It's a whole week in Nepal learning about red pandas!' I said. 'All you have to do is sign the permission form. Easy-peasy.'

'I'm not sure,' Mum said. 'Nepal is very far away, darling. It's in Asia. A whole other continent!'

'But it's only for one week,' I said. 'And I'd get to see a red panda! You know how much I love animals!

'I do,' Mum said. 'Tell you what, let's go to this assembly together first and find out more.'

'Red pandas are endangered, you know!' I said, crossing my arms. 'This might be my **ONLY CHANCE** to see one!'

'That's a bit dramatic,' said Mum, laughing.

'That wasn't dramatic. This is dramatic,' I said, and I flung myself on to the sofa. Our cat Marigold licked my nose. It tickled and I giggled even though I was trying hard to be serious.

Update, in bed
Just now, when Mum came in to kiss me good night and tell me to turn off the light, she said that if I did go to Nepal, she'd miss me very much ... and that means she's considering it!

School, Monday the next week, after assembly

Do you like exploring?

Do you care about animals?

Do you enjoy being in the outdoors?

Then join the Adventure Club this spring! Travel to exciting locations, see wild animals in their natural habitat and learn conservation skills.

Those were the words projected on to the wall when we got to assembly. And guess what? I love **ALL** those things!

Assembly had started with a woman with a friendly smile and short black hair standing up in front of us. A hush swept over the audience.

'I'm Julia,' she said. 'I'll be one of the leaders on the Adventure Club trip this spring. We have a whole team.'

Behind her, a new slide showed up on the wall:

Meet the Team

Julia: passionate about teaching and leading young adventurers. Medic.

Pema: has lived in the mountains her whole life and works to protect red pandas.

Rikesh: leads expeditions into the mountains.

Steve: Adventure Club vet.

Julia flicked through more slides, showing us pictures of red pandas sleeping on branches (they were sooo cute!), people riding yaks, and mountains.

'There are fewer than ten thousand red pandas

today and their population is declining,' Julia said. 'Can anyone tell me what a "habitat" is?'

Before I could think twice about it, I flung my hand into the air, wiggling my fingers. 'Pick me,' I said under my breath. I usually would have been nervous about answering a question in front of so many people, but I wanted Julia to see that I would be **PERFECT** for the Adventure Club because I already knew lots about animals.

Julia met my eyes and nodded at me. 'Yes?'

'A habitat is where an animal species lives,' I said in my best loud and clear voice, my heart pounding as everyone turned to look at me.

'Exactly,' said Julia, smiling at me. Mum gave me a proud hand squeeze and Julia went on. 'The two biggest threats to red pandas are a loss of their habitat and poachers who hunt them for their beautiful coats.'

I gasped at the thought of poachers. They sounded **TERRIBLE**!

'On the trip, our lucky adventurers will learn how to protect red pandas.'

I squeezed Mum's hand back in excitement. I wanted to do everything I could to help those red pandas. I wanted to be in the Adventure Club.

Home, later that same evening

We were barely through the front door when I asked Mum if I could apply.

'Julia seemed really nice,' I said. 'And the pictures looked amazing.'

Mum guided me to the couch and sat down with me, stroking my hair. 'I know you want to go, but Nepal is so far away. It's a nine-hour flight and then a trek through the forest. If you felt homesick you wouldn't be able to come home easily.'

'I'm already miles away from all my friends and

Dad,' I said. 'I'll miss you – and Marigold, of course. But I'll be OK.'

Mum looked thoughtful. 'Is this something you really want to do?' she asked finally.

I quickly nodded about seventeen times.

She nodded. 'OK. In that case, you can apply. I spoke to Dad last night and he agrees too.'

I threw my arms around Mum and hugged her tightly. Then I did a victory dance around the sitting room, dragging a string for Marigold to chase behind me.

After the excitement wore off though, I felt

anxious. Mum had said yes, but that didn't mean I was in the Adventure Club. There was still one big obstacle in my way.

The Third Adventure

Objective: Win the Adventure Club competition by writing about an adventure I've been on.

Obstacles: My adventures aren't fun enough, or exciting enough ... or even adventures at all!

But I still had to try! Sitting at the kitchen table, I read the Adventure Club competition guidelines that they'd given us at assembly. There was just one question:

Describe an adventure you've been on and tell us why you should be part of the Adventure Club.

I got a pen and some paper, and began.

I haven't been on any adventures before, which is why I **REALLY** want to go on this one.

That wasn't right – they wanted me to describe an adventure, not say I hadn't been on one. I scribbled it out and started again.

Once, in my old house, Mum accidentally locked us outside. The bathroom window was open but she couldn't fit through, so I had to climb in and unlock the door from the inside.

No, that wasn't exciting enough. I scribbled it out too. My answer had to be perfect.

I laid my head on the table. This was tougher than I had thought it would be. Marigold jumped on to the table and pressed her paws into my arm, purring and nuzzling against me.

'What's wrong, darling?' Mum asked me.

'I don't know what to write,' I said, lifting my head. And I let out a sigh so big it blew my hair out of my face.

Mum sat down next to me and read the question.

'It's not fair,' I said. 'How can I answer this? I've never had an adventure.'

Mum looked like she was about to call me dramatic again, so I frowned to make sure she knew I meant business.

'Why don't you write about moving house?' she said. 'We drove for six hours across the country with all our belongings and a cat! That was an adventure.'

I chewed the end of my pen and thought about it for a while before writing:

I've never been on an adventure in the mountains, but a few months ago, my mum, my dad, and I moved across the country. I had to carry heavy boxes up and down the stairs all day, which I guess was sort of like climbing a mountain.

I've also never seen a red panda, but when we drove to our new house, I held Marigold my cat in her carrier on my lap and even though she cried and meowed the whole time, I stroked her and fed her treats to calm her down and whispered that it was going to be OK. Mum said that I was very patient with her, and it was sort of like caring for an endangered animal, because there's only one Marigold.

I've never explored a different country like Nepal, but when we arrived in our new town, I explored the new house. Everything was new and unfamiliar, but it was also exciting, like exploring a new environment would be. I've never travelled away from home without Mum and Dad before, but I think I'm brave enough to. Mum said it took lots of courage to go to a new school by myself with new people and new teachers. Even though I was scared, I went anyway.

Even though moving to a new house was an adventure, I'm ready for an even bigger one. These are all the reasons why I think I should go to the Adventure Club.

Julia had said that we could add drawings. I covered the margins in drawings of red pandas until there was hardly any space left.

'Looks wonderful!' said Mum.

It didn't feel wonderful.

'Everyone else will probably be writing about how they went surfing or to France or something like that,' I said, suddenly feeling extra nervous.

'But that's their adventure and this is yours,' said Mum. 'Only you can write about this one and that's what makes it special.'

'OK,' I said. At least I liked my drawings.

I'm staring at my work now and I can't believe I actually finished it!

School, Tuesday, the next morning
I've just submitted my essay. I blew on the pages to give it extra good luck. And when I handed my work to Ms Perry, I crossed my fingers and toes.

Home, later that day
'If I get chosen for the Adventure Club, can you help me find an adventure outfit?' I asked Mum as I looked through my clothes.

'Of course, darling,' she replied.

'It has to be green like the trees and waterproof in case it rains and the jacket has to have a picture of a red panda on the back.'

Mum laughed even though there was nothing funny about what I'd said. I drew a picture like this for her to look at.

'I'm not sure we'll be able to find a jacket with a panda on the back. But we'll see what we can do,' she said.

Next, I wrote a list of everything I would need to pack ...

My Adventure Kit
- Adventure outfit
- Raincoat
- My notebook and pencil case
- My lucky mascot Poppy (my toy cat)
- Map
- Emergency snacks (cereal bars, a jam sandwich and a banana)
- Water bottle
- Torch
- Change of clothes
- Sun hat, sun cream and sunglasses

Friday, at home on the couch

Today was a **VERY BIG** day — and was so busy that it's almost bedtime and I haven't had a single chance to write in my notebook until now! All week I've barely been able to focus, waiting for the announcement of the winner. It's been worse than waiting for Christmas!

This morning, we all gathered in assembly. I sat down next to Charlotte. We'd been sitting together all week, talking about red pandas and sharing facts. I grinned at her and crossed my fingers.

She smiled back and crossed her fingers too.

'I'm very pleased that today we can announce which student will be going to Nepal,' said Ms Perry. 'This person wrote about doing something very brave in their essay ...'

I held my breath.

Ms Perry continued. 'And they are someone we recently welcomed to the school ... Tilly Corrigan!'

My mouth dropped open.

Charlotte whooped and clapped next to me. 'Stand up!' she whispered.

'No way,' I whispered back. Everyone was cheering and staring at me and I didn't know where to look. I definitely didn't want to stand up.

'Congratulations, Tilly!' said Ms Perry, waving at me. 'You're going to Nepal! Stay behind after assembly for a photo.'

Ms Perry then moved on to talking about the rainy weather and how we had to be extra careful on the walkways. I was SO relieved I didn't have to stand up until after assembly when everyone would be leaving the room. I lifted my shoulders and grinned – I couldn't believe that I'd really won.

After assembly was over, Ms Perry took a

picture of me holding a certificate decorated with red pandas. I smiled the biggest smile **EVER** for my photo. Ms Perry said the picture would be in the school newsletter! It's going to look like this ...

For the first time, I felt like I was really part of the new school. I was happy we'd moved.

When I got home, Mum hugged me so tight she lifted me into the air. Then we went to get ice-cream cones to celebrate. Mine was chocolate with sprinkles.

Marigold won't get off my lap as I write this. I think she knows I'm going away. I'll have to give her extra cuddles before I leave.

On an aeroplane! Ten days later

It's been a busy week getting ready but today Mum and I finally met the Adventure Club leader, Julia, and the other adventurers at the airport. When we arrived, everyone else was already there. There was one boy, one girl and both their parents. I smiled at them, wondering if they were as excited as I was.

The girl stuck her hand out. 'Hi, I'm Anita.'

She had straight black hair and a big smile and held a clipboard.

'I'm Tilly,' I replied. I felt

more confident about talking to people after becoming friends with Charlotte.

'I'm Leo,' said the boy, shaking my hand too.

He had short blond hair and clutched his backpack. He looked a bit nervous.

'I love your jacket. Is that a red panda on it?' asked Anita.

'Yeah!' I said. As a surprise Mum had sewn a red panda patch on to my jacket to complete my adventure outfit.

'That's sooo cool,' said Anita, examining it. 'We should all get matching ones!' Then Anita asked, 'What adventure did you write about to win? I wrote about how I organised my whole class to plant trees.'

'I wrote about the time I found an injured dog,'

said Leo. He smiled as he remembered it and looked a little less nervous.

'I wrote about how I moved house with my cat,' I said, feeling proud.

I could tell we'd all be best friends in no time.

Julia gathered everyone round and ran through the checklist.

Passports ✓
Walking boots ✓
Raincoats ✓
Warm clothes ✓
Day bags ✓
Socks ✓
Underwear ✓
Sun hats and warm hats ✓
Toothbrushes and toiletries ✓

'I've got binoculars and a compass too,' said Anita.

'That's wonderful, Anita,' said Julia.

'Are you nervous?' Leo asked me, whispering.

'A little bit,' I replied. 'How about you?'

'A little bit,' he said.

Mum knelt and gave me the biggest hug, cupping my head in her hands.

I squeezed her back tightly.

'I'll miss you,' said Mum. There were tears in her eyes as she pulled back. 'We'll talk every day, OK?'

I nodded, feeling a little bit sad too.

'Have a wonderful adventure,' said Mum.

'Do cats have good memories?' I asked, suddenly worried.

'I don't know. I think so. Why?'

'Please tell Marigold I love her every day and that I'll be back soon. She might forget me otherwise.'

Mum laughed. 'Don't worry, she won't forget you. But I'll tell her every day, just in case.'

Mum ruffled my hair. For a second, I didn't want to let go of Mum's hand. I pulled Poppy, my toy cat, from my bag, tucked her under my arm and felt better.

'Everyone ready?' asked Julia.

'I'll go first!' said Anita, lining up behind Julia.

We followed Julia through the airport. I turned and saw Mum waving at me and blowing me kisses. I kept turning back and waving until I couldn't see her any more.

Leo hung his head and sniffed.

'Do you need a hug?' I asked quietly.

He nodded.

I put my arm around his shoulder.

'Thanks,' he said.

'Mum said that we could go home at any time,'

I said, trying to sound reassuring.

'My dad said that too,' he replied. 'But I'm worried about flying. I've never been that high up before!'

'Think of the cool views we'll see though!' I said. He smiled again. Just a little one.

Now we're on the plane about to take off and I'm showing Leo my adventure notebook so he won't think about how high we're going to be. He said he liked my red panda drawings!

The Fourth Adventure

> **Objective:** Travel a quarter of the way around the world to Nepal.
>
> **Obstacles:** Being travel sick. Having to spend hours and hours and **HOURS** on a plane.

In a different airport (in India!)
I feel **TERRIBLE**.

We had to change planes in India and after the first plane I am **NOT** feeling very adventurous. I didn't sleep. I didn't watch any good films. I didn't even get to see any cool views because it was dark. As we stepped off the plane, I rubbed my tummy. I felt sick. I missed Mum.

'Perhaps walking will help,' said Julia, looking concerned as she led us through the airport.

But the walking didn't help.

I wish I was back at home.

On the Adventure Club jet, miles and miles in the sky, 5 hours later
I feel great now. Even better than great. I feel **FANTASTIC**!

That's because when I saw the next plane, I forgot all about missing Mum. My tummy even stopped churning.

The plane was painted in green tiger stripes, with animal faces covering the tail of the plane and birds on the wings. **THE ADVENTURE CLUB** was written in big swirly letters on the side.

It looked like this ...

'Welcome to the Adventure jet! Our eco-friendly aeroplane,' said Julia proudly.

'How is it eco-friendly?' I asked.

'It runs off fallen leaves,' said Julia. 'We're very busy collecting them in the autumn.'

Inside, we sat down in a row of comfy chairs.

'I bet this plane goes really fast,' said Leo, sounding a little nervous still.

'I hope so!' replied Anita.

'I can't wait to get there and meet the red pandas!' I added. Even Leo looked excited at that.

I stared out of the window as we took off, watching the ground below get farther and farther away. Soon, we were in the clouds and the whole plane was surrounded by whiteness. Then, suddenly, we were above them! I couldn't believe how high we were! The clouds looked like horses galloping through the sky.

'I love flying,' said Anita. 'What do you think the place we're staying will be like?'

'We're going to be high up on the mountain,' said Leo. 'Maybe there will be a giant slide to get to the bottom!'

'Maybe there will be so many red pandas that we'll see them every day,' said Anita.

'They're very rare,' I said. 'But I bet there will be all kinds of animals that we've never seen before.'

I glanced out of the window again and saw mountains below us.

'I think we're almost there!' I said, bouncing up and down in my seat.

Now Julia is handing out boiled sweets, which she calls toucan travel sweets, for landing. Mine tastes like lemon sherbet.

Day one, Nepal

I'm writing this from a whole other country. I **CAN'T BELIEVE** I'm really in Nepal!

As soon as we walked out of the airport I saw snow-capped mountains in the distance.

'Look at all that snow!' I said.

'It's beautiful!' said Leo.

'It is. But it looks very cold,' Anita added matter-of-factly.

'Here's the Adventure Club minibus now,' said Julia. 'Everyone in!'

The minibus had a painting of a red panda on the side of it. The driver parked and got out.

'I'm Rikesh, the expedition leader,' he said. 'I'm so happy to meet you all!'

Rikesh was wearing a thick-rimmed round hat, blue clothes and wellies, and had a moustache.

We got in and I wound the window down as we drove off into the city. The air smelled like pine trees and deep-fried chips. The roads were busy with cars, motorbikes and bicycle taxis. We drove through narrow streets, past houses, temples and palaces. The buildings were much more colourful than at home. All around were multicoloured flags fluttering in the wind on rooftops and hanging in the trees. I even saw some big gold statues!

My stomach felt queasy, possibly from the snacks I ate on the plane and possibly because I was starting to feel nervous again.

'Where are the red pandas?' asked Leo, looking out of his window.

'We have to drive out of the city and up to the mountains to see them,' said Julia. 'We'll meet Pema and Steve there. Pema grew up alongside the red pandas and will show us the work she's been doing to protect them. Sound good?'

'Sounds good!' said everyone.

Stray dogs slept on the side of the road.

'Look, monkeys!' said Anita.

'Where?' I asked, turning.

She pointed out of the left side of the van where there was a group of monkeys grooming each other on a flat roof. They were covered in short, brown fur with cute, swishy tails.

I forgot about being nervous and got so excited that I stuck my head out of the open window to get a better view. The air rushed past my ears.

And **THEN**, I saw a **CHEEKY** monkey slide down a tree and steal an apple from a fruit stall. It looked just like this...

'Put your head back inside!' said Julia from the front seat.

I pulled my head in and danced in my seat.

As we drove out of the city, birds of prey with huge wingspans flew low above the fields. They were longer than my neighbour's chocolate Labrador! Soon the road curved upwards and we entered the green foothills of the mountains.

Already I can't wait to tell Mum about all the animals I've seen here in Nepal. I'm going to have to stop writing because I'm feeling car sick but this is going to be the **BEST** week ever!

A few hours later, in the mountains
The mountains here look just like the pictures ...

As we got higher and higher in the minibus, the road became bumpier and bumpier. We entered a thick bamboo forest.

'How much longer?' asked Anita.

'We're almost there,' said Julia, turning round to smile at us.

The minibus slowed as we reached a clearing in the forest. Julia hopped out to yank open a fence and Rikesh drove through, approaching a wooden cabin in the middle of the clearing. To the left of it, I glimpsed tents. The minibus stopped underneath a giant banner with **THE ADVENTURE CLUB HEADQUARTERS** written on it in green.

'Welcome to the Adventure Club!' said Julia, opening the minibus doors for us.

We all sprang out. All around us were the sounds of chirping birds and humming bugs. The sky was the bluest I had ever seen – as bright as a felt-tip pen.

A big, long-haired dog barked at us.

'This is Mr Fluff,' said Julia. 'The Adventure Club dog. He's very friendly.'

I reached down to pat his head and he wagged his tail.

'Woah, those cows are **GIGANTIC**!' said Leo, pointing at some animals in a field to the right of the cabin.

'They're not cows,' I said. I recognised them from the book about mountain animals. 'They're yaks!'

I know because cows look like this:

And yaks look like this:

One of them was a silvery colour, almost the colour of storm clouds. I walked up to it and lifted my hand to its face. It sniffed me loudly and met my eyes. My hand trembled with excitement as I stroked the soft fur above its nose.

The Fifth Adventure:

    Objective: Touch a real-life yak.

    Obstacles: None. I did it!

'Momo likes you,' said Julia. 'You can ride her at some point if you want.'

I smiled. 'Yes, please!'

How **AMAZING** will it be to ride a yak!? I'm supposed to be helping unload the minibus but it's all I can think about!

Adventure Club headquarters, the mess room, 3pm
Just wait until I tell you about Club HQ! There are three buildings and I'm in the mess room which is where we'll meet, eat and relax. The inside walls are lined with tree trunks that climb up the walls and branches that stretch across the ceiling. The ceiling has big skylights in it that look out to the clouds. In the spaces between the trees the walls are decorated with photographs of red pandas, monkeys, yaks and mountains. There's a big board, which says:

The Adventure Club Rules

→ Leave no person behind.
   Adventurers stick together.

→ Go where you haven't gone and do
   things you've never done.

→ Expect the unexpected and be alert.

→ Care for people, animals, and the
   environment.

Pema met us inside. She was wearing turquoise
earrings, a fluffy red scarf around her neck and
khaki-coloured clothes.

'Welcome!' Pema said. We all introduced
ourselves – and then I noticed that Pema's scarf was
moving! Anita's eyes went wide as she saw it too.

'Your scarf just moved!' said Anita.

'It's not a scarf, it's a red panda!' said Rikesh, laughing. 'She was stolen from the forest and sold as an exotic pet but we rescued her and now she lives here, mainly outside. She was injured badly but she's recovered now and we're hoping one day in the future we can train her to live alone again in the forest.'

'We've named her Khushi,' said Pema. 'It means happy and joyful!'

I watched, mesmerized, as the red panda leapt down from Pema's neck and scampered up to an open window. She made a twittering sound like a bird as she perched on the windowsill and chewed on leaves.

'What's she eating?' asked Leo.

'I think it's bamboo,' I replied, recognising the shape of the stalk from the book I'd read in the library back at home.

'You're right,' said Pema. 'They eat the shoots, the stalks and the leaves. We make sure there's plenty of bamboo growing outside for her.'

'Are red pandas really becoming extinct?' I asked.

'Their population is declining, but we're trying to stop them from disappearing,' said Rikesh.

'Take a seat while I get us some refreshments,' said Julia, pointing at some big couches in the centre of the room. 'You can talk about why we're all here.'

'To protect the red pandas!' I said, sitting down beside Leo and Anita.

'Exactly!' said Rikesh, sitting down on a couch across from us. 'Let me tell you a bit more about them, so you can understand why it's so important we protect them. I'll start with one of my favourite things about them. You know how animals belong in different groups, or families? For instance, big cats are one family. Can anyone name some members of the big cat family?'

'Lion,' said Leo and he did a roar.

'Leopard!' I shouted.

'Cheetah!' said Anita.

Rikesh nodded. 'Very good. Now, can you guess which animal family the red panda belongs to?'

'The bear family!' said Anita. 'Like a panda bear.'

'Maybe it's part of the cat family too?' I suggested, thinking that Khushi looked as graceful as a cat.

'I bet it's related to a fox!' said Leo. 'It's the same colour!'

'Those are all brilliant guesses,' said Rikesh. 'But the answer is that the red panda belongs to its very own family. They're completely unique.'

'And red pandas live alone,' added Pema. 'They each have their own area, about the size of a square mile. We know that there's one living not far from here and we've seen evidence there might be a second! Some people think there are fewer than a thousand red pandas in the wild in Nepal, so these two are very important.'

Leo, Anita and I all beamed at each other. That meant that our job for this week – looking after those two red pandas – was very important too!

'This week you're going to help us on patrol,' said Pema. She held up a sign. 'This is what we do on patrol.'

She handed us each a smaller copy of the sign to keep. I've put mine on the next page.

Red Panda Patrol

→ Look for red pandas and for signs that they're around. You might see droppings, paw prints or foraging marks.

→ Make sure their habitat hasn't been damaged and they have enough bamboo to eat.

→ Check for signs of poaching. You might find traps and snares.

→ Record everything and add it to the database.

The meeting ended, Julia brought in snacks and now I'm eating a banana and watching Khushi scampering around the branches above us. I **CAN'T WAIT** to go on my very first red panda patrol!

Outside Adventure Club mess room, a few minutes later

We've just had a tour of the Adventure Club HQ, Mr Fluff leading the way. I drew a map of the area.

We visited the vet clinic and met Steve the vet. He had a friendly smile and was as tall as the sunflower I grew last year!

Then we saw the yak enclosure, the firepit and the tents. Finally, Julia led us to an orange-painted building, close to the tents. Outside stood two sinks.

'This is where you can wash your hands and brush your teeth,' said Julia.

Then she showed us inside the building, where there were toilets. Well – sort of! There were two cubicles with holes in the middle of the floor, each with a toilet seat placed around the hole. There was a bucket filled with sawdust and a spade resting on top next to the seats.

'It's a compost toilet,' said Julia proudly. 'You put the sawdust down the hole when you're finished.'

I peered down into the hole. I expected it to smell terrible. There was a **LONG, DARK** drop down but it didn't smell bad at all! I'm actually very excited to use it!

HQ, Inside the mess room, 5.30pm
I'm back in the mess room, next to a big table covered in metal dishes filled with rice and different coloured curries.
Or what's left of them.
Before we ate the curries, they looked like this ...

When we sat down, I noticed that the table was decorated with strings of orange marigolds. At first, they made me think of Marigold the cat, which made me miss home, but then I spotted

Khushi the red panda in the branches above us, and realised she looked a bit like Marigold! She could be my Marigold replacement while I was here. I watched her climb down a branch headfirst. I remembered reading that red pandas have thumbs to help them in the trees. Khushi stopped on a wide piece of wood and curled up to sleep, wrapping her tail around her like this ... She looked even more like Marigold now!

Even though my favourite food is pasta with

lots of cheese, and there was nothing like that here, the dishes were all really tasty, especially a soup called lentil dal. It was **DELICIOUS**!

After dinner, Julia led us out to the balcony. We drank hot chocolate and watched the sun set over the valley. Bats flitted around us.

'Are they vampire bats?' asked Leo, sounding worried.

Julia shook her head. 'No, they're mouse-eared bats and are harmless to humans. They eat insects.'

'Oh,' said Leo, looking pleased. 'Good.'

'I could stay up ALL night and watch the bats,' I said. 'I'm not tired.'

'Me neither,' said Anita. 'I'm far too excited to sleep.'

'Well, we should try and go to sleep soon,' said

Julia, grinning at us. 'You have a very busy day tomorrow and it's best to get on the new time schedule so that you're not jetlagged.'

'What's "jetlagged"?' asked Anita.

'It's when you struggle to adapt to a new time zone,' said Julia. 'Right now, back home in England, it's lunch time, so that's why you might not feel tired. But here in Nepal, it's bedtime.'

That's when I realised that dinner time in England would be midnight here! What if I get hungry in the middle of the night? I guess I do have my emergency snack bag. Mum had made me remove the banana, she said it would get squished, but I still have the cereal bars. **PHEW!**

HQ, the mess room, a few minutes later
Guess where I'm sleeping tonight? Julia just showed us

and it's going to be **INCREDIBLE!** But first let me tell you about how I spoke to Mum.

'Who wants to ring home?' asked Julia after we'd finished the hot chocolate, holding a phone.

We all stuck our hands in the air. I went last. Julia helped me dial Mum's mobile.

'It's ringing,' I whispered.

'Hello?' said Mum on the other end.

Even though I knew she was miles and miles away, hearing her voice in my ear made it feel like she was close by.

'Hi, Mum! It's me. We're here!'

'Hello, darling! It's lovely to hear your voice. Is it fun? Is everyone friendly?'

'It's the best,' I replied. 'I'm going to be an adventurer for ever. And guess what? There's a red panda right here in camp! I'm going to put you on the phone to her.' I held the phone up towards Khushi and just as I did, she let out a squeak in her sleep. I waited for a few more moments in case she did it again, but she was silent, so I brought the phone back to my ear. 'Did you hear her squeak? What did you say to her?'

'I told her about how I'm so proud of my daughter.'

I beamed from ear to ear. 'It's so much fun here. Oh, and Mum – can we get a compost toilet please?'

'I'll have a think about it,' said Mum, laughing.

We talked for a bit longer and then Julia said it was time for bed.

'I'll call again soon, Mum. I love you.'

'I love you too, darling.'

I was about to hand the phone to Julia when I remembered one last thing. 'Don't forget to hug

Marigold for me!' I shouted down the phone.

Then Julia said, 'So for sleeping we have two options. You all can sleep in here,' she pointed to the back of the mess room where there were some bunk beds. 'Or you can sleep outside in the tents.'

'Let's go and see the tents!' I said, jumping up.

They were **HUGE** and arranged in a circle with a firepit to the side.

'We can stargaze if we sleep out here!' I said.

'And we can tell ghost stories,' said Anita.

'I don't like ghost stories!' said Leo, shivering.

'We can tell campfire stories then,' I suggested.

'And we could have a midnight feast,' he said thoughtfully.

'I take it you choose the tents, then?' asked Julia, smiling.

'**ABSOLUTELY!**' we all said.

I'm grabbing my backpack from the mess room now to move in to my tent!

My tent, a few minutes later
I'm all cosy and snug curled up in my sleeping bag under the mosquito net. It's dark now, so I have a torch.

Julia let us each pick our favourite tent and I chose the one closest to the fence. Outside, it's painted with stars and inside are solar-powered fairy lights. It's way better than the one we put up in my garden once that sagged in the middle.

'My tent is just behind all of yours, next to Rikesh's, Pema's and Steve's,' said Julia. 'If you need anything at night you can call my name and I'll be right there. And there's a bell you can ring if it's an emergency.'

I inspected the metal bell tucked into the side pocket of the tent.

We all brushed out teeth and went to the toilet, then got into our tents. After a few minutes, there was a shout from the tent next to me.

'What is it?' I asked, rushing out with my torch. Anita had scrambled out of her tent too.

Leo appeared at the entrance to his tent, looking alarmed. 'There's a **SCORPION** on my bed!' he said.

'Oh wow, can I see?' I asked, going over and climbing inside to look. Anita followed me in but stayed behind me.

A big scorpion, the size of my hand, was curled up on Leo's pillow.

This is its ACTUAL size!

'What's wrong?' asked Julia, sticking her head inside the tent. 'Is everyone OK?'

'There's a scorpion on my pillow!' said Leo. 'I don't want to sleep next to something with a stinger!'

'You're actually very lucky to see this,' said Julia, ducking into the tent to join us. 'These scorpions are also endangered. Does anyone want to help me remove it?'

'I do!' I said.

'Why don't you find a safe spot for us to release it?' asked Julia. 'Under a rock would be good, that's where they like to hang out usually. This one must have just wanted a little nap somewhere more comfortable!'

It was my first real wild animal encounter in Nepal – and now I had a special assignment!

Objective: Find the scorpion a safe spot.

Obstacles: It's hard to find a rock in the dark. And a bit scary!

I left the tent and searched the area outside with my torch. I spotted a giant stone resting against a smaller rock near the edge of the clearing.

'Here!' I called. 'I think this rock is perfect.'

Julia, Anita and Leo appeared at the door of Leo's tent. Julia held the scorpion in a glass.

'I thought I was going to get stung,' said Leo, who sounded calmer now that the scorpion was contained in a glass. 'Aren't they poisonous?'

'No,' replied Julia. 'But it would have hurt! Check your beds before you get in at night in case there are any more.'

Julia placed the glass down on its side and we all watched as the scorpion crawled out of it and quickly scuttled under the rock.

'We've had our first animal adventure together!' I said.

Anita and Leo laughed. 'I'd rather the next one didn't sting,' said Leo.

I think I'm going to check my sleeping bag for scorpions one more time before I try and sleep!

My tent, a few minutes later
All clear! Now I just have to go to sleep ...

The Seventh Adventure

    Objective: To sleep in a tent outside.

    Obstacles: Not feeling tired AT ALL.

The sounds at night here are different to the ones at home.

Things I can hear:

- The rustle of my sleeping bag
- Snoring from someone's tent — I can't tell who
- The trees blowing in the wind
- An owl
- Crickets chattering to each other
- Mr Fluff barking

Even though I'm not the teensiest tiniest bit sleepy, I'm going to close my eyes so I can listen harder ...

Day two, my tent

I'm so excited — we're about to go on a mountain trek to track red pandas! I'm supposed to be packing my day bag, but I wanted to write down everything that happened this morning before I forget a single detail.

77

The day started with Julia's voice waking me up.

'Good morning!' called her singsong voice from outside my tent. 'Rise and shine, adventurers.'

I opened my eyes. I couldn't believe I'd slept through the **WHOLE** night! I hadn't even thought that I was tired. It was cold and I reached for my woolly hat and pulled it down over my ears. I didn't want to get out of the sleeping bag.

'Breakfast is ready!' said Julia.

I huddled down further into my sleeping bag.

'And then we're going on a red panda patrol.'

That made me sit up.

'OK!' I replied. 'I'm awake!'

Outside, it was sunny but cold. The sky was blue and clear. The trees gently blew in the wind around us. Rikesh and Pema waved good morning.

Anita was already out of her tent. She had on so many layers of clothes she looked like a grizzly bear, and she was sitting on a big rock with her eyes closed, basking in the sun like a lizard.

'Hi,' I said to her as I approached. 'Are you wearing two hats?'

'I hate being cold,' she replied, wrapping her arms around her body.

'You'll warm up soon,' said Julia, handing us mugs of hot lemon tea.

Leo joined us, rubbing sleep dust from his eyes and yawning.

For breakfast, we ate hot porridge with raisins. By the time we'd finished the air was a little bit warmer. Anita pulled off one of her woolly hats. Khushi was eating her breakfast too, sitting in a tree. She used her front paws to put bamboo shoots in her mouth. Afterwards she cleaned her fur by licking it, just like Marigold does. I wanted to stroke her, but Julia said it was important she didn't get too used to humans or she would find it hard in the wild.

'Today we're going to try and confirm that there is a second red panda living close by,' said Julia. 'To get to the patrol area we have to trek over a mountain pass. Although it's sunny today, it will be cold up there.'

'Oh no!' said Anita. 'Not more being cold.'

The Eighth Adventure

Objective: To climb over a mountain pass.

Obstacles: It's really high up and far away. There might be snow. It's going to be exhausting.

'Are we going to Mount Everest?' asked Leo.

'We're in the Himalayas, which is the same

mountain range, but we're not near Mount Everest,' said Julia.

Then she told us all to pack our day bags.

I can hear Anita and Leo talking outside, so I had better hurry and finish getting ready!

The mountains, an hour later

Wow, trekking is hard! We're taking a break before crossing the mountain pass, so I thought I'd use that time to update this notebook — you won't believe what just happened!

When we left camp this morning, we immediately set off through the forest. Many of the trees were covered in red, purple or pink flowers. Butterflies fluttered around us. Julia and Pema were at the front and Rikesh was at the back. Leo, Anita and I were right in the middle. Steve stayed behind to work in the vet clinic. Mr Fluff padded along beside me.

We turned a corner and the path got steeper and steeper. We all slowed down a bit. It was tough work climbing up a mountain.

'Are we as high as the Eiffel Tower?' asked Anita.

'Are we as high as Big Ben?' asked Leo.

'Are we as high as an aeroplane?' I asked.

'We're higher than the Eiffel Tower and Big Ben but not as high as an aeroplane,' answered Julia, stopping to pick up a fallen red flower off the ground. She tucked it behind her ear. 'Soon we'll be a mile and a half above sea level.'

'Wow,' I said. Foothills covered in green forest stretched out below us and in front of us stood big, snowy peaks.

'How long have we been climbing?' I asked.

'About an hour,' said Julia.

'Is that all?' I asked. I couldn't believe it. It felt like we had been walking **ALL MORNING**.

'Look at how far you've come in that short amount of time though,' she said.

I looked behind us. She was right – I couldn't even see the Adventure Club headquarters!

As I turned back to look at the path ahead, I noticed a black dot in the distance. It was heading down the mountain towards us.

'What's that?' I asked.

The fast-moving black dot was getting closer and closer.

'That's a yak!' said Julia. 'And it's stampeding!'

'Everyone out of the way!' yelled Rikesh, grabbing Mr Fluff's collar.

The yak was galloping straight towards us, with no sign of slowing down. Julia pushed me up against the side of the mountain along with the others. I flattened myself as much as possible.

The thunder of the yak's hooves beat against the path.

My breath was fast and loud.

The yak hurtled past us. It was so close I could see its eyes flicking wildly about and smell its fur. Then it was gone.

'Everyone OK?' asked Julia after a moment.

Mr Fluff barked.

'That was so exciting!' said Anita.

'That's why one of the Adventure Club rules is to expect the unexpected, isn't it?' asked Leo.

'Exactly!' said Julia. 'Let's take a little break before we cross the mountain pass. We need a minute to recover from our yak encounter!'

I think seeing the yak was probably the most exciting adventure that has happened to me so far.

The mountain pass, an hour later

We made it over the mountain pass! The 'pass' is the path between the high peaks of a mountain. But as we were crossing the pass, something scary happened. The scariest thing that's ever happened to me.

As we climbed higher and higher, there were fewer and fewer trees and suddenly the ground ahead was white. This was the kind of snow I've only ever seen in films – all sparkly and fluffy. Pema, Julia and Rikesh stopped to check the map.

Leo, Anita and I looked at each other, grinned, and then raced into it. It crunched and squeaked under my feet.

I wrote my name in the snow with the tip of my toe. Anita joined me and wrote hers next to mine.

I added *The Adventure Club* underneath.

'Leo!' called Anita. 'You have to write your name too!'

He ran over and added his name in curly letters.

'Let's make a snow child,' I said to Anita and Leo.

Anita clapped her hands together excitedly.

'Let's make a snow red panda!' said Anita.

'Yes!' said Leo as he gathered snow.

The Ninth Adventure

Objective: Make a snow red panda.

Obstacles: It's freezing!

We made a ball for the body, pushing it across the ground so that it picked up snow as it rolled, getting bigger and bigger, until it was as high as my waist. Then we made a smaller ball for the head. It took all three of us to lift it off the ground and balance it on top of the body.

After that we moulded some of the top ball into ears and carved out a long bushy tail along the ground. I dug deep into the snow and found two pebbles which were perfect for eyes. Then I noticed some pine needles that had got caught in Leo's day bag.

'We can use these to make whiskers!' I said.

Julia was watching and when we were done,

she added the flower from behind her ear to make the nose.

We all stepped back to examine our snow red panda. It was **AMAZING**.

'What should we call it?' I asked.

'Let's call it Winter,' said Anita. 'It can be our snowy mascot.'

Julia took out her camera to take a group photo of us with the snow red panda.

'Everyone say, "Adventure Club"!' she called.

'Adventure Club!' we all said.

The camera clicked.

Anita's teeth started to chatter. 'I'm **FREEZING**!' she said.

Rikesh said, 'Let's move on. Our destination is just down on the other side of this snow – it'll be a bit warmer there.'

It was icy on the way down the pass. As I edged carefully behind Leo, my foot slipped and before I could catch myself I was **SKIDDING DOWN THE PATH** like a sledge!

I slid past Leo and all the way past Pema, who tried to grab me. I sank to my knees to stop myself from falling over but I was still sliding fast, close to the edge of the path. There was a big drop on the other side of it.

'Tilly!' shouted Leo.

'Hold on, we're coming!' shouted Pema.

'**I CAN'T STOP**!' I shouted. The edge of the cliff was getting closer and closer.

I jammed my foot into the snow, slowing myself down a bit. I scrabbled at the snow with my hands, trying to find something to hold on to.

Suddenly, I stopped. Someone had caught my hand, just before I reached the edge.

'Are you OK?' Pema asked, helping me to my feet.

'Yeah,' I said, though my heart was still pounding. I didn't want anyone else to know how scared I had been. I brushed the snow off my coat. 'That was kind of like skiing, wasn't it?'

'Does anywhere hurt?' asked Julia, appearing and crouching down in front of me.

I shook my head.

'I thought you were going to tumble over the

edge!' said Leo, clambering through the snow toward me.

'I knew you'd all stop me,' I said, although my arms felt shaky. Perhaps I was still a teensy bit scared.

We set off again, down the mountain pass. From then on, I stared at my feet as I walked down the mountain, careful to check where I stepped. I didn't want to fall over again.

We're resting on some boulders now and if I'm totally honest, I'm still feeling a little shaky from my almost-fall over the cliff. I guess adventures can be dangerous. But it'll be worth it if we see the red pandas.

Red panda territory, 11am
We're finally in the area where the wild red panda might be living! There's no more snow, just green forest. Tall

trees stand all around us and thick stalks of bamboo grow underneath them — exactly the kind of habitat red pandas need. I can't stop looking around for one!

'Time for an Adventure Club team meeting!' Pema said when we arrived.

We all sat down in a circle. I could barely sit still I was so excited!

'We have a few rules,' said Rikesh, once we were all settled. 'One: it's important that you don't wander off. Stay close. Two: if we tell you to do something, do it right away. We're deep in the forest and there could be an emergency. Three: it's important that we're quiet. We don't want to disturb the red panda. Does everyone understand?'

We all nodded.

'Brilliant!' said Rikesh. He handed us each a

sheet of paper. 'Now for the fun part. One of the main ways to know that a red panda is in the area is to find its droppings. That sheet of paper will help you identify them.'

I looked at the piece of paper. It had drawings of different types of poo.

Yak poo

Red panda poo

Bird poo

Leopard poo

'There are other ways to track a red panda,' said Pema, 'for instance, we can examine bamboo for bite marks and look for paw prints. But today we'll mainly be searching for the droppings. Are you guys ready?'

'YES,' we all said.

The Tenth Adventure

Objective: Track a red panda. And hopefully see one!

Obstacles: They live in a large area. They are excellent at camouflaging. This is going to be **TRICKY**.

Rikesh and Pema took the lead, with Anita, Leo and me behind them, followed by Julia at the back. We crept through the bushes, pushing ferns out of the way and stepping over fallen tree trunks. At first, I searched the trees for flashes of red above me. But then I remembered that I was supposed to be looking for droppings.

There were lots of brown things on the ground.

It was hard to spot any droppings. I did see:

- Brown leaves
- Brown twigs
- Lots of mud
- A brown millipede (He was really cute!)

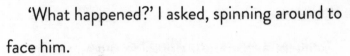

Leo gasped.

'What happened?' I asked, spinning around to face him.

He pointed down at his foot.

He had stepped right in a pile of droppings.

I held out the piece of paper in front of me to compare. They definitely looked like red panda droppings.

'Oh well done!' whispered Pema. 'That's it. That's red panda poo.'

I pretended to high five Leo from a distance, not wanting to make an actual clapping sound –

or to step in the poo myself!

Pema grabbed a stick and prodded the droppings, opening them up in the middle.

'It's fresh,' she said. 'See how it's wet and green on the inside?'

I nodded, though I didn't get too close. A few flies buzzed around the droppings and Mr Fluff sniffed them.

'Yuck,' said Anita, wrinkling her nose.

Pema crouched down next to us.

'That means that there's probably a red panda very close by,' she whispered. 'If we're really quiet then we might be able to see it. It might even be in the branches of the trees above us.'

We all immediately looked upwards.

'Let's set up an observation spot,' whispered Rikesh. 'Somewhere we can sit comfortably and watch.'

He went over to a tall tree with a thick trunk.

'Here will be good,' he said.

While he set up the observation spot, I opened my notebook. I **HAD** to draw that millipede before it disappeared!

But now I'd better go — I don't want to miss the red panda!

Observation spot, an hour later

Rikesh told us to sit in a circle around the tree, with our backs resting against the trunk. That way, we had all directions covered. Then, we waited.

Turns out, waiting for red pandas to appear takes **AGES**! We were sitting for so long that I almost fell asleep. Birds chirped and sang all around us. I had to get out my notebook again to keep me awake.

I felt fidgety and looked beyond the trees at the clouds. The sky was filled with the best kind of clouds, the big fluffy white ones.

'Do you think that cloud looks like an alligator?' I whispered to Leo next to me, pointing.

'I think it looks like a dragon,' he replied. 'And that one next to it looks like a giant doughnut.'

I giggled. 'I could eat a giant doughnut right now.'

'Shhh,' whispered Anita. 'I'm trying to look for the red panda.'

I sighed. I was getting bored of waiting.

Things I wish I was doing instead of waiting:

- Whistling to all the birds around
- Climbing the trees
- Shouting and hearing it echo off the mountains

But instead of shouting or climbing, I'm staying quiet and watching the branches, searching for the tiniest rustle. It turns out that adventuring is actually a bit boring sometimes. Or maybe I'm just not very good at it. At least I'm staying quieter than Mr Fluff though, who's been snoring — **OH MY GOD!**

Update, a few minutes later

A gigantic flying bug had landed on my arm. I **HATE** flying bugs.

And as soon as I saw it, I couldn't help it, a scream left my lips.

A scream so loud that the birds shot out of the trees.

The bug flew off, and headed straight for Leo. It got tangled up in his hair. Leo shrieked and leapt into the air, jumping up and down. The bug landed on the ground and scurried under a leaf.

'What's wrong?' asked Julia, hurrying over. 'What happened?'

I stared at my boots, feeling like I'd ruined everything. I'd definitely scared off any red pandas that were near.

'A bug flew at me,' I said quietly. 'I'm sorry. I didn't mean to make a noise. It was just really, **REALLY** big.'

'Don't worry,' said Julia. 'These things happen.'

'We can try again after lunch,' said Rikesh. 'I'm hungry.'

'Me too,' said Anita.

But I could tell they were just trying to make me feel better. It didn't work – I felt awful – like I had just ruined any chance we had of seeing a red panda.

Lunch spot, 1pm

Over lunch I thought about how I could make it up to everyone. Next time, I would make sure that the red panda couldn't see me at all. I thought about some of the ways that animals stay hidden and realised that mostly it's because they're camouflaged. Here are some examples:

- Leopards have spots that hide their outline, especially in forests with light and shadow.
- Tigers have stripes to blend into tall grasses or forest undergrowth.
- Red pandas have red and white markings that help them blend in with the brown branches and red tree moss.

I realised that we needed some camouflage of our own. We were going to be on the ground among green leaves and brown trunks. I had an idea ...

Lunch stop, 30 minutes later
I think this has been my best idea yet!

Half an hour later, I stood back to admire my work. Anita's face was covered with brown and green spots that I'd drawn with my colouring pens. She looked like a leopard.

I'd drawn stripes on Leo's face so he looked like a tiger, and then they'd each drawn red panda markings on me.

'Are you ready to track the red panda again?' asked Pema.

'We're ready,' I said.

We definitely looked like adventurers now.

Red panda area, 3pm

Guess what? My camouflage worked!

Once we got back to the red panda area I focused as hard as I could on being silent. Anita looked through her binoculars next to me.

After a few minutes, she tapped my arm and pointed excitedly. I followed her line of sight and a movement caught my eye. I stared at the tree where it was coming from. There was something up there, walking and balancing along the branch.

A red animal with a bushy tail!

Leo gasped and alerted Julia and Rikesh. Soon everyone was watching it.

The red panda reached the end of the branch and stopped, staring straight at me. My heart raced. It had bright eyes and white markings on its face below fluffy ears. It almost looked like it was smiling. I tried to talk to it with my eyes.

We're not going to hurt you. Don't be scared.

Then the red panda stuck out its tongue. I'm pretty sure it was the coolest moment of my **ENTIRE** life. All the boring waiting had been worth it.

After a few seconds, it scurried off, over the tree branches out of sight.

It was all I could do not to yell with happiness.

In the mountains, a few hours later

My feet are tired and my legs are sore and we're still an hour away from the HQ.

'We're taking a slightly different route back,' Pema said, as we set off from the red panda territory. 'We need to check for any signs of poaching or habitat loss.'

But when we reached the area she wanted to check, Pema stopped. Something was wrong, I could tell right away. I ran to catch up to her. In front of us was a huge clearing. All the trees had been chopped down and the bamboo was cut and trampled.

'What happened?' I asked, shocked at the sight of all this destruction in the middle of the forest.

'Illegal logging,' said Pema, with a grim expression. 'People come into this protected area and chop down the wood for timber.'

'And the red pandas need the bamboo?' I asked.

She nodded. 'They can eat over twenty thousand leaves a day! They need the bamboo forest to survive.'

Rikesh snapped photographs and marked the area on his map.

'We're always planting new bamboo to replace plants that have been cut down illegally,' said Rikesh. 'We can plant some more tomorrow. It will take a while to grow, but it'll give that red panda that we saw a chance to survive. If you are all up for helping, that is?'

We all nodded. I knew that we would do whatever we could to help the red panda have enough to eat.

Day three, Adventure Club HQ

This morning, I woke up super early, ready to go and plant bamboo. When I crawled out of my tent, I saw that Anita and Leo were awake and dressed too. Khushi was curled up, asleep on a big tree branch. She scratched the fuzzy hair on her face.

'She's so cute, I wish that I could hug her,' said Anita.

'Me too,' I replied.

Khushi's long whiskers twitched in her sleep.

'I wonder what she's dreaming about,' said Leo.

'Probably bamboo,' I said, and they laughed.

'Morning!' said Pema, emerging from her tent. 'I thought we'd ride the yaks there this time. It'll be quicker and give us more time to plant the bamboo once we're there.'

We jumped up quickly. I'd never even ridden a horse before and now I was going to ride a **YAK**?

This was the best trip **EVER**!

The yaks stood in their enclosure. Rikesh put leather saddles on their backs, placed over brightly patterned blankets, and harnesses over their necks. The yaks lifted their huge heads and stared at us as we approached.

I noticed a big board on the outside of the fence. It had a picture of each of the yaks and said:

Meet the Yaks

Momo: long, silvery coat with a white star on her forehead.

Makalu: black and white coat with a black stripe down his face.

Annapurna: brown, fluffy coat like a teddy bear.

'They're all named after mountains – except Momo, who ate a momo off my plate once,' said Pema.

'What's a momo?' I asked.

'A delicious dumpling. You'll get to try those later in the week.'

'They must be good if Momo the yak likes them!' I said.

'Has anyone ridden a horse before?' asked Pema. 'It's very similar to that.'

'I have!' said Leo, throwing his hand into the air.

'I rode a donkey once!' said Anita.

'I haven't,' I said quietly.

Leo and Anita would know exactly what to do

and I had no idea how to ride any kind of animal!

'That doesn't matter,' said Pema to me, noticing my worried expression. 'It'll be everyone's first time riding a yak!'

The Eleventh Adventure

Objective: To ride a yak.

Obstacles: Not falling off.

'Can I ride Momo?' I asked.

'Can I ride Makalu?' said Anita, jumping up and down on her toes with excitement.

'And I want to ride Annapurna,' said Leo. 'He just licked my hand!'

Rikesh helped Anita sit on Makalu, Julia helped Leo on to Annapurna, while Pema led Momo over to me.

'Hi, Momo,' I said. 'My name's Tilly.'

Momo softly snorted in response and let me stroke her neck.

Pema linked her fingers together to form a platform with her hands and told me to step on them. I did, and gripped the top of the saddle. Pema lifted me up higher and then instructed me to swing my other leg over the side.

'I'm up! I made it,' I said.

I patted Momo's fur. I couldn't believe it. I was really riding a yak!

'Now listen, everyone,' said Pema. 'I'll give the command for the yaks to go and then they'll start walking. They'll walk in a line. Momo likes to be in the front.'

'Fine by me!' I said.

'If you want to stop, say "rok", firmly. It's the Nepali word for stop. Everyone got that?'

We all nodded.

'Let's practise then,' said Pema, and she made a clicking noise with her tongue. The yaks immediately started following her. Momo took the lead.

I felt very high up. Gradually I got used to the sway of motion as Momo walked. I gripped her sides tightly with my knees. It took a lot of concentration.

After we'd done a whole lap of HQ, Pema said we were ready for the mountains!

The mountains, a few hours later

So far today has been **AMAZING**. Just wait until you hear why! Although there was a bad bit as well. I'll tell you about that too ...

After packing our adventure bags, we left HQ and rode the yaks along a narrow path through the trees. It wound around the mountain, getting higher and higher. After a while, I felt brave enough to glance behind me at the others. They both looked completely relaxed on their yaks. Leo was gazing around at our surroundings. Anita only had one hand holding the reins.

I tried to hold on with only one hand like Anita, but I wobbled and quickly grabbed the harness again.

Soon the ground became uneven and rocky. In the distance, I could see a clearing in the trees not too far ahead of us, and a big lake. Suddenly I saw a flash of movement against the rocky cliff on the other side of the lake, a blur of white with black spots.

I squinted, trying to see better. The animal paused for a second. I could make out a long tail. I held my breath. Could it really be a snow leopard?

Everyone else was chattering, unaware.

'Look,' I whispered.

'What?' asked Pema.

The snow leopard turned its head towards us for a split second. Its mouth opened in a flash of pink.

I gasped.

The snow leopard leapt through the air, then bounded over the jagged edges of the cliff until it was out of sight. A few small stones tumbled down after it. It was gone in a flash, like it had never been there.

'Everything OK, Tilly?' asked Pema.

I nodded. It happened so quickly I almost couldn't believe it. But on the inside, I was dancing. I had just seen a snow leopard.

(That was the best bit of the day.) The snow leopard looked like this:

We walked on. As we got closer to the lake, Momo sped up. She must have been thirsty after all the walking.

'Stop,' I said, trying to remember the Nepali word.

But Momo didn't understand me. She hurried faster and faster towards the lake. The path began to slope sharply downhill and I slid forwards on her back.

'Tilly!' shouted Pema.

I fell against Momo's neck and lost my balance. I slid down

down

down

and hit the ground with a thud. (This was the worst bit of the day.) I lay there with my eyes shut for a minute. I imagine it looked a bit like this:

'Tilly!' shouted Pema again.

I opened my eyes and stared up at her worried face.

'Are you OK?' asked Pema.

'Does anywhere hurt?' asked Julia, coming up and kneeling beside me.

Momo had stopped. She swung her huge head round, as if to check on me too. I sat up carefully. Luckily, I'd fallen on to grass. My elbows were grazed, and I felt shaky, but nothing was hurt. Adventuring was hard!

'I'm OK,' I said, holding my hands out for them to help me up.

Pema and Julia pulled me to my feet.

'Let's take a break for a few minutes,' said Rikesh.

Together, we walked over to the lake. We helped Rikesh lay out a picnic blanket, while the yaks grazed the grass on the bank.

We all sat down on the blanket. The lake rippled and reflected the clouds and the mountain peaks in it.

'That looked scary,' whispered Anita. 'I'm glad you didn't get hurt.'

'Would you like my crisps?' asked Leo.

I smiled at them both. 'Thanks. I'm OK, though.'

After the snack and water break it was time to keep riding again. Butterflies gathered in my tummy as I approached Momo.

'You can walk with me if you don't want to get back on,' said Pema.

I shook my head. 'I want to try again.'

I took a deep breath and climbed back into the saddle, trying not to think about the fall. I felt better once I was on Momo's back.

We set off again. Now we were heading deep into the forest. We passed tons of cool things as we rode:

- Long-tailed birds
- A pheasant with iridescent feathers
- A deer looking up at us through the trees
- Purple flowers on trees
- The secret snow leopard!

'You're doing great,' said Pema to me. 'I can tell that Momo likes you. Not everyone would have got back on after falling off, but you did. Well done.'

'Mum says that I'm very determined,' I replied.

Pema laughed. 'I can see that.'

After a while, Rikesh stopped ahead and shouted, 'We're here!'

All the yaks halted and I almost tumbled off again.

So, today I rode a yak **AND** I saw a snow leopard. And the day's not even over yet!

Bamboo forest, three hours later

The Twelfth Adventure

> **Objective:** Plant a bamboo forest.
>
> **Obstacles:** Finding good soil to dig in. Making sure the bamboo is well-planted.

We've just finished planting the new bamboo forest for the red pandas.

When we arrived, we were each given a spade. Our first job was to dig holes. Then we placed the bamboo plants in them, filled the holes with soil and patted the earth tightly around them to make sure that the bamboo didn't fall over. Anita had planted trees before, so she led the way.

After working for a few hours, we'd planted fifty bamboo plants. We stood back to admire our work.

'Thank you for your help!' said Pema. 'In a few years you can come back and see how big the plants have grown.'

I hope that I can come back some day and see them. We only have a few days left and I'm not at all ready to leave!

Adventure Club HQ, after dinner
We're sitting around a **HUGE** bonfire. The moon and stars shine above us. If I tilt my notebook towards the flames, I can just see enough to write.

Earlier, we collected wood kindling while Rikesh

built the fire.

'My arms are sore from carrying the bamboo,' said Leo, as he picked up a stick.

'My legs and back are stiff from riding the yaks,' added Anita.

'Me too,' I said, even though some of my aches came from my fall.

As we brought the wood to the firepit, we heard the adults talking quietly.

'I haven't seen a tiger like that in a while,' said Steve.

We all stopped in our tracks.

'Beautiful!' said Pema.

'Should we tell the kids?' asked Julia.

'No,' said Rikesh. 'There's no point – it's gone.'

I look at Anita and Leo, eyes wide.

'Did they say what I think they said?' asked Anita.

'A tiger? Here?' asked Leo, looking around us.

I tried to remember what I had read about tigers and the local area.

'I didn't think tigers lived in this part of the mountains any more,' I said.

'Maybe it got lost,' said Leo.

'Maybe,' I said with a shrug.

We walked back to the firepit. The grown-ups were now talking about the red panda we had seen.

'The red panda looked healthy,' said Pema.

Rikesh nodded, stirring the fire with a long stick. The orange flames curled and sent sparks flying into the sky. We all sat down on camp chairs around it. Mr Fluff wound in and out of the chairs, so that everyone could pat him.

'Did the red panda really stick its tongue out at us, or did I imagine that?' I asked.

Pema laughed. 'I saw that too. Red pandas smell

the air with their tongues. It was probably smelling you.'

Steve sat down by the fire holding a guitar and quietly played some chords.

'We should make up an Adventure Club song!' I said.

'Yes!' said Leo and Anita.

We worked on it for the rest of the evening, until it sounded something like this:

Have you heard about the Adventure Club?
Make new friends from around the world, hooray!
Why don't you join the Adventure Club?
Explore new places and travel the yak-way!
Welcome to the best-ever club
Where adventures happen every day!

'We can sing it when we get back home to

remember our trip,' said Leo.

I imagine sharing the song with Charlotte when I get back to school. She'll love it!

Day four, HQ, the mess room, 4pm
Today was **NOT** a good day. It was almost as bad as the time I thought I'd lost Marigold. It started off well ...

In the morning, Mr Fluff curled up on my feet as I ate my porridge and toast by the still-warm fire with Julia and Pema. I wondered if I could convince Mum to get us a dog. It could be our at-home adventure. It wouldn't

have to be a big dog, just big enough to sit on my feet like Mr Fluff. I wasn't sure whether Marigold would like it though.

Anita was the last one to wake up. She had a scarf wrapped around her neck that was so fluffy you could barely see her face poking out.

'I hate being cold,' she said grumpily, joining us by the fire.

'We know,' I said and giggled.

The moon was still in the sky even though it was daylight.

After we'd eaten, we helped feed the animals, starting with the yaks, who were in their enclosure. Momo recognised me instantly and trotted over to say hello. I couldn't believe that I'd ridden her yesterday. It almost felt like a dream. I held my hand out flat and she licked grass off my fingertips with her rough tongue. It tickled. We left a big pile of grass in the corner for them to munch on.

Next, we fed Mr Fluff his dog biscuits and watched Pema check there was enough bamboo growing for Khushi. The red panda was sitting in the stalks, stripping the shoots and nibbling on them.

Then Pema called us all over.

'Today we're going to monitor a special red panda,' she said. 'She's called Iniya, which means "sweet", and she's going to have cubs this year! In a month or two. We'll ride the yaks again as it's a bit far to walk.'

I took a deep breath. I was going to ride Momo again – and this time I would nail it.

A few minutes later, Julia was helping me get settled on Momo.

'All right up there?' she said, and winked.

I nodded firmly.

Once she left to help Leo on to Annapurna, I leaned forwards to whisper in Momo's ear.

'Today we're going to master this riding thing,' I said. 'We can do this.'

Maybe my pep talk with Momo worked or maybe I was getting more confident – either way, I felt relaxed as we headed out.

We followed Pema in single file, scanning the area all around us.

I soon spotted an animal footprint by a muddy puddle.

'Here!' I said, and we all stopped and crowded around it.

'That's not a red panda print unfortunately,' said Rikesh.

'Does it belong to a leopard?' asked Leo.

'Or a monkey?' asked Anita.

'It's a deer,' said Pema. 'See, you can make out

the outline of its hoof there.'

I nodded, disappointed it wasn't a red panda paw print. Still, it was early. We had lots of time.

But hours later, we still hadn't found anything.

Not one paw print.

Not one bite mark.

Not even a piece of poo.

But then I spotted something that I didn't want to find. The worst thing ever to find in red panda territory!

A metal trap, glinting in the sun.

'Stop!' I shouted. 'Look.'

'Poachers,' said Rikesh under his breath.

Rikesh, Pema and Steve went over to the trap, took off their jackets and rolled up their sleeves.

'Don't worry,' Pema said. 'We're trained in dismantling traps.'

My skin prickled. 'Why do poachers want the

red pandas so badly?' I asked.

'For their beautiful red coats,' said Pema sadly. 'Or to sell as pets.'

All I could think was how **AWFUL** it would be if the poachers had got the red panda we were looking for. We had to find a sign of her. I had to know that she was still here.

Pema and Rikesh finally dismantled the trap. They packed it carefully away and we set off again in search of Iniya. We looked for hours, scanning every tree and patch of undergrowth for anything that would tell us that a red panda was near. In the end, Pema signalled to us to stop.

'It's time to head home,' she said.

'We haven't found Iniya yet!' said Leo, dismayed.

'I'm going to stay here overnight on the lookout for poachers,' said Rikesh. 'Tomorrow you can come back and help me search again.'

'But that's dangerous!' I said. 'If the poachers come you might get hurt. The rules say adventurers stick together. And I **REALLY** want to help!'

'You are helping,' said Pema gently. 'And tomorrow you'll help some more.'

We were silent on the way back home. I could tell Anita and Leo were as worried about the red panda as I was. All the way home I thought about Iniya, out there somewhere, being hunted by people who wanted to hurt her.

My tent, 8pm
Tonight, my tent doesn't feel as cosy as it normally does, even though I'm burrowed deep in my sleeping bag, writing this by torchlight.

When we got back from our trek a few hours ago it was almost dark. We had a quick dinner and then Julia let us choose postcards to send home. I picked one with a picture of a yak on the front. We all wrote them in the mess room as we drank hot chocolate and ate biscuits. This is what I wrote:

Hi Mum,
The last two days have been the best ever. I rode on a yak called Momo **AND** we saw a red panda.

Today something bad happened though. We went looking for a red panda called Iniya, but we found a trap set by poachers. I'm **EXTREMELY** worried about her now. I hope we can find her and that she hasn't already been caught by the poachers.

I wish you and Dad were here so that I could show you

everything. Can you read Dad this postcard?

Love, Tilly
P.S. I think we should get a dog.
P. P. S Don't forget to give Marigold a hug every day from me.

'You're very quiet tonight,' said Julia, as she collected my postcard. 'Don't worry, Rikesh is keeping an eye out for Iniya.'

I smiled a little.

'Are you tired?' Julia asked.

I nodded.

'Me too,' she said. 'I think it's time for all of us to go to bed. Tomorrow is another day, and you need to be full of energy to track Iniya.'

So I brushed my teeth quickly and got right into my sleeping bag.

Maybe it was because I'd just been writing to Mum, but I suddenly felt homesick. I wanted to be curled up with Marigold, in my warm home. I wanted to be eating pasta and cheese and reading a book with Mum.

Instead, I was in the middle of nowhere, far away from everyone. Well, everyone except Poppy. I gave her a good cuddle.

Things I miss about home:
- My mum
- Marigold
- My bedroom

Thinking about home is making me miss it even more. There's still three whole days to go!

My tent, late at night

I was trying not to cry but a little whimper came out. And then, I heard a rustling outside. I suddenly remembered the tiger the grown-ups had been talking about. What if it was coming to eat me? I pulled the sleeping bag over my head and stayed very, very still.

Then I heard the sound of the zip being lowered. I didn't think that a tiger would bother with a zip when it had huge claws that could tear my tent into pieces, so I peeked my head out of my little nest.

It was Anita. Phew.

'Are you OK?' she asked. 'I thought you might need cheering up?'

'Thanks,' I said, and I smiled at her.

'I brought my emergency sweet supply too,' she said, offering me a gummy worm.

'Hey, are you having a midnight feast without me?' came Leo's voice from outside. He climbed in. 'I brought chocolate.'

'I have some cereal bars somewhere,' I said, rummaging in my day bag.

'Yum!' said Anita, as she dug into the chocolate.

Leo shone the torch at the side of the tent and made a shadow puppet snake with his hand.

I laughed and added a flying butterfly.

'Does this look like a cat?' asked Anita, as she twisted both her hands together in front of the torch.

I squinted. 'A little bit,' I said. 'Maybe more like a cow?'

We started giggling.

There was a rustle from outside.

'Shh,' I said. I hoped we hadn't woken up Julia.

The rustling grew closer and louder.

'What is that?' asked Anita, eyes wide and scared.

'Maybe the yaks broke out of their enclosure and came to see us?' said Leo.

But then there was a sniffing noise outside the tent that didn't sound anything like the yaks.

'What if it's a bear?' whispered Anita. 'Are there bears here?'

I thought back to the book about Nepal I'd looked at in the library. I remembered seeing pictures of black bears and brown bears. My heart thumped loudly. Then I remembered the tiger again. None of those options sounded good.

'Let's wake up Julia,' said Leo. 'Where's the bell?'

I grabbed the bell from the tent pocket but didn't ring it.

'Hang on,' I said. 'I'm going to look first.'

'Are you sure that's the best idea?' asked Anita.

I nodded, although I wasn't really. 'I want to see what's out there.'

The truth was that even though I was scared, I wanted more than anything to see a bear or a tiger.

I gave Anita the bell and she clutched it, ready to sound the alarm.

I took a deep breath and slowly unzipped the top of the tent flap.

I raised my right eye to the hole and stared out. It took a second for my eyes to adjust to the darkness.

'What is it?' asked Anita, her voice trembling.

I saw the outline of an animal, sneaking between the tents. I squinted. It was too small to be a bear or even a tiger. Maybe it was a bear cub?

Then I heard a bark. 'It's Mr Fluff!' I said and unzipped the tent all the way.

Mr Fluff bounded into the tent. Anita threw her arms around his neck and hugged him.

'He was probably feeling left out with us three in here,' she said.

'You did give us a fright though, didn't you?' Leo told Mr Fluff.

I didn't say anything. Most of me was relieved, but a little part of me was sorry not to have seen a tiger.

After we finished the snacks, Anita and Leo left, but with Mr Fluff next to me, it feels almost like I'm back home in my bed with Marigold and I don't feel homesick any more. But now I better get some sleep! I can't be tired tomorrow. We **HAVE** to find Iniya the red panda and make sure she's OK.

Day five, Adventure Club HQ, morning

I'm sitting with the yaks, yawning. I'm tired but **NOTHING** is going to stop me from finding Iniya.

There was a storm in the middle of the night and everything was damp and soggy, so we ate breakfast inside this morning. Khushi padded along a branch above us on all fours, her white ears pointing forwards at the sound of our voices. From below I could see her furry feet too. I could watch her for hours and hours and never get bored. She looked like this ...

Pema brought us some sweet papaya and mango, but she wasn't her usual chatty self. She didn't even offer any extra red panda facts when I said that red pandas have strong paws and sharp claws to climb the bamboo stems.

In fact, everyone was silent and worried. I knew it was because of the missing red panda and the presence of the traps and the poachers.

I looked up at the trees in the distance and hoped with all my might that we would find some sign of Iniya today.

The Thirteenth Adventure

Objective: Find Iniya, the missing red panda.
Obstacles: She could be anywhere. Or ... she might have already been taken by the poachers.

After breakfast, we went to the yak enclosure.

Momo came over to me and grunted a greeting.
I fed her a handful of grass, rubbed her forehead
and stared into her large dark eyes.

I don't feel nervous or scared yak-riding any more. All
I care about is finding the red panda safe and sound.

Red panda territory, after lunch
We met up with Rikesh after lunch.

'I scared off some poachers in the night but I
haven't found Iniya,' he said.

We all glanced at each other. I couldn't believe
there were poachers **RIGHT HERE** last night. I'm
glad Rikesh was there to make them leave.

We were all **EXTRA** careful and quiet as we
hunted for any sign of Iniya. Pema and Rikesh had
a map which they used to mark the places that
we'd searched. Everything was muddy and damp

after the rain. We dismounted the yaks to examine the ground.

But by the late afternoon we hadn't seen anything.

No droppings.

No paw prints.

No bite marks.

Then there was a rustling above and my heart leapt with excitement.

A grey monkey swung through the trees ahead.
Behind it followed about
twenty
more, all
travelling easily
through
the forest.
Above us, the forest
was suddenly alive with

movement. Monkeys bounced on branches and swarmed over the trunks.

'Wow!' said Leo, eyes wide with wonder.

We perched on the edge of a trunk and watched them. The monkeys stripped some of the leaves off the branches and ate them. They chattered to each other.

'What do you think they're saying?' I asked.

'I think that one's saying, "I found a great leaf",' said Leo.

'And that one's saying, "all right, there's no need to shout about it",' added Anita, and we laughed.

'See that one over there?' whispered Rikesh, pointing at a giant monkey with a white fluffy mane, sitting very high up at the top of a tree and looking around. 'He's keeping lookout and will let the others know if there's danger nearby.'

The monkeys were cool, but I was too worried about Iniya to enjoy watching them! I closely examined the ground one last time for droppings. I spotted a line of ants running up and down the trunk of a tree, a heart-shaped rock, and even a tiny purple frog sitting at the edge of a puddle. But no droppings.

'Have we looked everywhere?' I asked Pema. I felt all sad and deflated, like an empty balloon.

Pema shook her head thoughtfully. 'There's one more place we could try,' she said.

'Phew,' I said. There was still hope!

She gave me a grin. 'There's just one catch. It's on the other side of a river!'

We rode on the yaks until we reached a river.

'I'll stay with the yaks in this clearing,' said Rikesh.

'I'll go first over the river,' Pema said, and she held her arms out to balance as she stepped on a large stone sticking out of the water. Then she immediately stepped back on to land. 'The stones are slippery! I don't think it's safe.'

'But I'm great at balancing,' said Leo.

'And I have extra grip on my boots!' said Anita.

After discussing it, Julia, Steve, Pema and Rikesh took all the bags across and then came back and stood in the river, which wasn't deep, so they could help guide us across. Leo went first with no problems.

Then it was my turn. Even though Steve said I could grab his hand, crossing the river was **SCARY!**

I held my breath as I placed my foot on the first stone. I wobbled and gripped on to Steve's hand to steady myself. After the first one I got used to the feeling of it and I almost ran across. I felt like a gymnast on the balance beam as I jumped from stone to stone.

I imagine I looked like this:

Too soon, I was over on the other side. 'Yes!' I said. 'I made it and I didn't get wet at all.'

Anita was making her way carefully across. Just as she put her foot out, a monkey screeched loudly. I jumped.

'Argh!' shouted Anita. She wobbled. Julia reached out for her, but it was too late. Anita slipped and tumbled into the river.

Julia scooped her out immediately and Steve and Pema helped carry her across to the bank.

'Anita!' I ran over and knelt beside her.

'Don't worry, I'm fine!' she said. But her teeth chattered. I remembered how much she hated being cold.

Julia draped an emergency blanket over her shoulders. 'I'm going to take you back to HQ to warm up,' she said firmly.

'B-but I want to find the red panda!' Anita said, shivering.

'I'm sorry,' Julia said sympathetically. 'We'll just have to wait for news.' Anita didn't want to go but she was shivering so much she couldn't say no.

With Rikesh's help, Julia carried Anita across the river on her back. Rikesh rejoined the yaks and Julia and Anita turned and waved to us before walking off. And then we continued our red panda patrol.

Pema checked her watch as we walked. 'Only half an hour before we have to turn back too,' she said.

'Why can't we stay out at night?' I asked.

'Yeah, Rikesh did it!' added Leo.

'Rikesh has had proper training. It's not safe for you,' replied Pema. 'It's harder to see in the dark and there are animals around at night that we don't want to meet.'

'Like what?' I said eagerly.

'Like snow leopards and bears.'

I smiled to myself. I'd **LOVE** to see my secret snow leopard again. I turned my gaze to the trees.

'Where are you, red panda?' I asked under my breath.

We spread out to do one last sweep of the area, and I spotted something on the ground between the bushes in the distance. It was a brown-reddish colour.

I held my breath. I had to get closer.

'Where are you going?' said Leo.

I put my finger to my lips and pointed at the bushes.

And as we parted the branches to get a better look, we saw her: the red panda, Iniya. But I knew immediately that there was something wrong. She tried to limp away from us, but collapsed on the ground.

And then I saw that her fluffy back paw was stuck in a trap. My heart ached at the sight of her trapped like that.

I spun around.

'Get Pema,' I said to Leo.

I didn't move any closer so as not to frighten Iniya.

'Don't worry,' I whispered to her. 'We're going to help you.'

Pema and Steve were next to me in an instant. Steve stepped forward and edged closer to the red panda. Iniya attempted to run away but the trap held her. She turned, trying to stand with both front paws raised in the air, claws extended.

Steve stopped moving. Pema emptied out her day bag and handed him a thick blanket. He gently covered Iniya's head.

'That's so she won't be scared,' said Pema quietly.

Steve examined Iniya's wounded leg and held her still as he removed the trap.

'It's a deep cut,' he said. 'We need to take her back to the camp.'

'You go on ahead,' said Pema. 'We'll meet you back at the HQ.'

Steve headed quickly back towards the river, carrying the wounded red panda gently in his arms. We watched until he was out of sight.

Now Pema's finished packing her day bag and we can leave. Around us the sky's getting dark. I hope Iniya's going to be OK!

Adventure Club HQ

We made it home, but the forest at night is **MUCH** darker than night time at home — it was a bit scary! Now I'm inside the mess room with Anita. She's bundled up in blankets and sipping hot chocolate. I've been filling her in on everything that happened after she left... It was an adventure even getting back!

The Fourteenth Adventure

    Objective: Get back to the Adventure HQ safely.

    Obstacles: It's getting dark.

We soon reached the clearing where we had left the yaks and mounted them.

'Everyone stick close together,' Pema said as we entered the forest. 'Follow me.'

Everything looked different in the dark. Flowers turned into strange shadowy creatures and branches looked like hands reaching down. I was very glad that Pema and Rikesh were with us.

'I'm not scared of the dark. I'm not scared of the dark. I'm not scared of the dark,' whispered Leo under his breath.

'Don't worry,' I said to him. 'I'm scared of the dark too. Let's sing a song.'

'How about the Adventure Club song?' said Leo.

'Perfect,' I replied, and we started singing. 'Have you heard about the Adventure Club?'

Soon Pema joined in, and finally Rikesh.

Crickets buzzed and chirped around us, like they were joining in too.

Once we started singing, the rest of the journey went by quickly.

'Well done on finding Iniya, Tilly,' said Pema as we rode. 'If you hadn't, I don't know what would have happened to her.'

My chest filled with pride. But I was too worried about Iniya to feel happy yet.

'I just hope she's OK,' I said.

There was a clatter and a shriek behind us.

'Tiger!' shouted Leo. 'Tiger!'

We all stopped and Pema and Rikesh leapt from the yaks, running over and shining their torches on Leo. I couldn't see any sign of a tiger, but there was a **HUMONGO-GIGANTIC** moth the size of my head tangled up in his day bag.

'That's not a tiger,' said Rikesh. 'It's an atlas

moth. They're very gentle. Just keep still for a moment...'

Leo stopped wriggling and Rikesh carefully freed the moth. It dropped to the ground, wriggling around and slowly flapping its reddish-brown wings.

'Is it OK?' I asked, bending over it.

'Yes, it fans its wings like that to scare predators away,' said Pema, pointing at its wings. 'See how the patterns and movements make it look like a snake?'

I nodded. It was the most beautiful moth that I'd ever seen.

This is what the patterns looked like:

'Let's give it some space to fly away,' said Pema. 'It looks a bit scared.'

'Sorry I panicked,' said Leo, waving goodbye to the moth.

We all stepped back and waited. A few moments later the moth took off and flew away into the night sky.

Leo bent and picked up his torch, batting away the bugs flying around the light.

'Why did you think it was a tiger?' Rikesh asked Leo, once we were moving again.

'We heard you talking about a tiger by the fire,' said Leo, hanging his head. 'We know you didn't want to worry us ...'

Rikesh and Pema burst out laughing.

'We were talking about a tiger butterfly!' said Pema.

'Wait,' said Leo. 'So there's no tiger?'

Rikesh shook his head, still laughing.

'I knew it couldn't be a tiger,' I said.

Just then, we saw, the lights of the HQ lighting up the darkness. We had made it home.

And now Iniya's being examined by Steve in the vet's clinic. I really hope she's going to be OK …

Day six, the vet clinic

I'm in the vet clinic and guess who's with me? … **INIYA!**

The first thing I did this morning was find Steve. I dashed up to him and asked, 'Is she going to be OK?'

'She was very weak – I don't think she would have survived another day of being trapped,' said Steve. But thanks to you, she'll be just fine!'

'Yes!' I said and I punched the air like a superhero.

'You can watch her as she wakes up,' he said. 'The cut wasn't as deep as I thought and she's strong enough to release later. And I've managed to put a tracking collar on her, so that we can monitor her movement from now on.'

'She'll never be lost again!' I said. '**HOORAY!**'

Steve took me to Iniya's cage. She was curled up, sleeping peacefully, with her tail wrapped around her body. I rested my arms on the cage and watched her. Her round black nose twitched and she scratched her ear with her fluffy paw. I remembered that red pandas had hairy soles on their paws. After a while, she sniffed and began to stir. Her eyes opened.

I knew if I was her, I would be scared to wake up somewhere new. I looked deep into her eyes and spoke gently.

'You're going to be fine. I cut my leg once too,

on a fallen branch in the woods. You're being very brave. Soon you'll be back at home.'

The red panda lifted her head and made a twittering sound as if she was talking back to me.

'I know it can be scary to be far away from home,' I continued. 'But you don't need to worry. We'll take you home soon.'

The red panda looked at me for a long moment, then she laid her head back down and shut her eyes, snuggling down again.

I'll never tell anyone this because I know they wouldn't believe me, but I just **KNOW** she understood every word that I said.

The mountain path, a few hours later
We've just dismounted from the yaks and I'm sad because I realised this will be the last time I'll ride Momo!

As we were riding to the red panda territory, I thought about all the amazing adventures I'd been on with Momo and wished that I could take her home with me. I wondered if Mum would let me get a dog and a yak. But then I realised a yak probably wouldn't like living in a flat.

When we dismounted, I wrapped my arms around Momo's neck and hugged her. She turned her head towards me and rubbed it against my leg.

'Thank you for being my adventure companion,' I whispered.

Steve was carrying Iniya in a covered cage.

The Fifteenth Adventure

Objective: Release Iniya into the wild.

Obstacles: Finding the perfect spot. Not wanting to say goodbye.

At last we reached the spot where we had found Iniya. We waited at a distance and watched as Steve placed the cage down. He opened it and then stood out of the way.

Iniya slowly climbed out of the cage. She looked around, sniffing, her tongue testing the air. She gave a little stretch. Then she bounded into the trees above us.

We all stared up at her and she stopped and gazed back, looking straight at me.

'Bye, Iniya,' I said. 'Stay safe.'

The red panda disappeared into the safety of the trees.

As we turned back, Leo asked, 'Do you think Iniya will eat the bamboo that we planted one day?'

'I'm sure she will,' said Julia. 'And who knows? One day you might return and see that bamboo forest for yourselves.'

Adventure Club HQ, my tent

Tonight is our last night at the Adventure Club —
and our last night sleeping in the tents. I'm really
going to miss the fairy lights and the cosy sleeping
bag.

Since it was the last night, Julia, Pema, Steve
and Rikesh threw us a party. They made yummy
foods like momos, which are dumplings filled with
vegetables. They're the food Momo the yak tried
to eat! Pema held a competition to see who could
draw the best red panda.

Mine looked like this:

Pema decided they were too good to pick one.

'They're all going up on the wall of the HQ,' she said.

'I don't want to leave tomorrow,' I said, when we were sitting around the firepit toasting marshmallows.

'You can always come back one day,' said

Pema. 'In fact, I hope you will.'

Khushi the red panda was sleeping on a branch on her tummy with her legs hanging down over the sides. She looked like she was smiling in her sleep, with her face pressed against the wood. I hoped she'd enjoy living in the wild when she got there.

Day seven, saying goodbye

The next day we packed and said goodbye to Pema and Rikesh and Steve and Khushi and Mr Fluff and the yaks. Then we set out off with Julia on our long journey home.

It took **FOREVER**.

Home

I can't believe I'm back home in England!

Mum met me at the airport. She held a sign that looked like this:

I rushed forward, ducking under the barrier, and threw my arms around her. Leo and Anita ran to their parents too.

After saying goodbye to everyone and swapping our addresses, we got in the car. Julia waved us off. As we drove home, I talked without stopping about all our adventures.

'Then we went into the forest and you'll **NEVER** guess what happened,' I said to her. 'We saw a real-life wild red panda! And then I found another one caught in a trap. It was **AWFUL**.

You've never seen **ANYTHING** like it. But we saved her and Steve the vet helped her, then we released her into the wild.'

'That sounds very exciting,' said Mum.

'I almost forgot, there was one night where the dog who was called Mr Fluff saved my life because there was a bear outside my tent.'

Mum whipped her head round. 'A bear?'

'Well,' I said sheepishly. 'There wasn't really a bear. I thought there was but anyway, I was thinking that we could get a dog. You know, in case of bears.'

'Let me get this straight,' said Mum. 'You want to get a dog in case there are any bears here, in England?'

'Exactly,' I said.

She smiled. 'I don't think bears are something we need to worry about, Tilly. Besides, what would

165

Marigold think?'

I sighed. 'I guess Marigold probably wouldn't like a dog,' I said.

I couldn't wait to see Marigold. When we got home I flung open the front door and called her name. She was sitting at the top of the stairs, but she ignored me.

'I think she's upset that you left,' said Mum, watching us.

Mum was right; Marigold was being all huffy and offended. 'I'll coax her out with a cat treat,' I said. 'And then I'll tell her all about my adventures too.'

The cat treat bribery worked! Now I'm curled up in my bed with Marigold next to me, purring. It reminds me of being with Mr Fluff. I wish he was here too! Then again, he might be too hot in my warm house with all his fur.

I wonder if he'll remember me. I know that I'll never forget him. Or the red pandas we met. Or Momo the yak. Or the secret snow leopard.

The Last Day of Spring

It has been a few days since I've written in here because I've been very busy writing to Leo and Anita but I just had **A GREAT IDEA.** I was watching a bumblebee outside the kitchen window when the idea popped into my head. I was so happy I shrieked out loud and scared Marigold off her spot on the window ledge.

First Day of Summer Term at School

The first day back at school is always exciting, but I think today was my **BEST** first day ever.

In the morning, as soon as I got in to school, I raced straight to Ms Perry to tell her about my idea. She listened carefully. Then she asked me some questions. I answered them as well as I could. She thought for a moment, then clapped her hands together and said, 'You know what, Tilly? I think that's a wonderful idea! Why don't you tell everyone about it in assembly this afternoon? We can write what you're going to say during lunch today.'

'Perfect!' I said. And then I remembered how many people would be looking at me in assembly. That didn't sound perfect **AT ALL!**

The Sixteenth Adventure

Objective: To tell the whole school about my adventure in Nepal and about my big idea.

Obstacles: Feeling nervous about standing up in front of everybody.

I had butterflies in my stomach as I stood there, waiting for assembly to start. But then I remembered that night in the campsite, hearing what I imagined was a tiger prowling around, and being brave enough to unzip my tent. And I thought of when Momo had bolted off, with me clinging to his neck, and how I had still climbed back on again. And I remembered when I had nearly skidded off the edge of a cliff and I hadn't given up. I had ridden yaks and crossed rushing rivers and rescued a red panda. When I thought of all that, I didn't feel scared any more. And when I saw Charlotte smiling at me from the front row, I suddenly couldn't wait to tell everyone about all my adventures.

I grinned back at her and began reading out my notes to the assembly.

'In Nepal, I stayed at the headquarters of the Adventure Club and I saw the most amazing animals. I rode a yak called Momo, a huge atlas moth landed on my friend Leo, and my group saw two different red pandas in the wild! In fact, we had to rescue one from a poacher's trap.

'Red pandas are very endangered because their habitat and food is disappearing. This got me thinking.' I paused and looked at everyone. They were listening intently. 'Some bees and butterflies right here at home are threatened because their habitat is disappearing too. So ...' I gave a dramatic pause. 'I thought we could start our own Afterschool Adventure Club! I want to create a bee and butterfly garden here, just like the bamboo we planted for the red pandas in Nepal. And we can even build our own Adventure Club headquarters here, at school!'

Ms Perry stepped back up to the podium now, just like we'd planned.

'We'll be having a meeting on Thursday about the Adventure Club for anyone who wants to join.' she said.

I can't wait for our first meeting — and to tell Leo and Anita all about it!

School, Thursday, 3pm

In class today, we learnt which plants are a good habitat for bees and butterflies. And we had the first meeting of the Afterschool Adventure Club to plan the garden. We met in the classroom as our temporary HQ. Lots of my class came and they all had really good ideas. It was decided that we would plant a willow-house (A willow-house is made by growing stems of willow from the ground, then weaving them together to make a den!) for our real HQ. We also came up with a plan for the bee garden.

Ms Perry said we could call it our 'manifesto' – which she said is a fancy word for a plan.

> **The Afterschool Adventure Club Manifesto**
>
> **Mission:** To create a butterfly and bee garden.
>
> **How:** Plant a wildflower meadow on the school field, with a hedgerow border of lavender, corn marigold and wild pansies, a herb garden and a willow-house HQ.

It's going to look **AMAZING**, just like this ...

We just need to get some bee-friendly plants, willow stems, compost and gardening tools and then we can start building it!

Garden Centre, Saturday, 9.30am

I woke up extra early this morning and ran to wake up Mum.

'Can we go to the garden centre to buy all the plants we need to start the bee and butterfly garden?' I asked, all in a rush.

Mum fumbled for her watch and looked at the time.

'Let's have a cup of tea first, shall we?' she said, yawning. 'The garden centre won't be open for hours!'

When Mum finally drove me there, I went right up to one of the nursery workers.

'We're starting an Adventure Club at my

school,' I told him. 'We're going to try and build a new habitat for the bees and butterflies and we need plants that they like.'

I held out the list that we'd drawn up at the meeting. The man looked at it carefully.

'We have all the seeds and plants you need,' he said. 'And I have some old spades that you can borrow. We'll deliver them to your school. You'd better buy some string too.'

'Perfect,' I said. 'Thank you!'

'Have you ever planted a bee garden before?' he asked.

I shook my head.

'If your school wants, I can come and teach you what to do?' he said. 'I'm Tim.'

'That would be **BRILLIANT!**' I said.

Tim took us round and filled our trolley with the plants we needed. He even threw in some extra

174

and then helped us load up the car.

'I'm proud of you,' said Mum, as she started the car.

I smiled. Everything was coming together! Operation Adventure Club was about to begin.

School, Wednesday, 5pm

The first proper Afterschool Adventure Club happened **TODAY!**

> **The Seventeenth Adventure**
>
> **Objective:** To start an Adventure Club at school.
>
> **Obstacles:** Being worried no one will show up. Having to plan adventures.

Charlotte, Ms Perry, Tim and I waited for people to arrive in the hall. I paced around, biting my nails, nervous that no one would show up.

For a second, I wanted to run home.

Then ... the whole class arrived!

'Thank you for coming,' I said shyly. I glanced at Ms Perry, who gave me an encouraging nod. 'We're here because it's not just animals far away that need looking after – we need to care for the ones in our own country as well. Now, shall we go and plant our garden?'

To my surprise, everyone clapped.

'This way,' Tim said to us, leading us out to the school field. 'We need to dig the soil over here to plant the wildflower meadow and we're going to plant the willow in a large circle over there.'

Everyone got down on their hands and knees and began digging.

After an hour Ms Perry brought out biscuits and juice and we all sat down in the shade to admire our work.

I couldn't stop smiling. The meadow would bloom with daisies, buttercups and clover and be filled with butterflies and bees. There was still plenty to do – like planting the hedgerow and the herb garden. But soon the willow-house will grow and be covered in green leaves. It will be the **PERFECT** place to have Adventure Club meetings.

I did miss Anita and Leo though. If they were here, it really would be perfect. Still, I'd sent them letters, so I hoped they'd respond soon.

I never imagined I'd get to go on any adventures. And now this notebook is full of them. I wonder what my next adventure will be ...

Hi Tilly,

I'm writing with some very exciting news! Iniya has had two cubs. The whole red panda family is doing well. Here's a pic!

Take care,

Julia

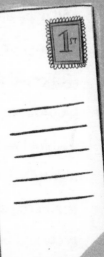

Hi Tilly,
It's Leo. I loved your Afterschool Adventure Club idea so much that we're going to do one too. Our school is going to make a butterfly garden!
Bye for now, Leo

Hi Tilly,
My teacher said that our class could come and visit your school to see the garden you all planted. How great is that? I can't wait to see you!
Miss you!
Anita

How to Build Your Own Bee Hotel

Did you know that there are 250 wild bee species in the UK? Many of these are solitary bees, which means that they live alone and not in a hive.

Solitary bees make nests in hollow stalks and holes. They aren't aggressive and very rarely sting, which make them the perfect guests for your bee hotel.

To build a bee hotel, you will need:

- A small terracotta plant pot (with holes in the bottom) or an empty 2-litre plastic bottle
- Modelling clay (optional)
- Approximately 25 bamboo canes, with the hole no bigger than 10mm in diameter
- String
- Scissors
- Ruler

- An adult (to help with the cutting bits!)

What to do:

1. If you're using a plastic bottle, cut the top off.

2. Draw a straight line along one side from the top of the plastic bottle to the bottom.

3. Measure roughly 7cm from the top and 7cm bottom along the drawn line and make a hole in the plastic bottle at each of these spots.

4. Thread the string through the two holes so that you can hang up your bee hotel when it's complete.

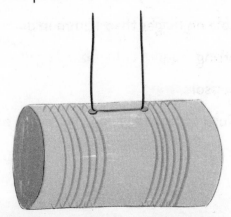

5. If you're using a pot, thread the string through the top and the existing hole at the bottom so that you can hang your bee hotel when it's complete.

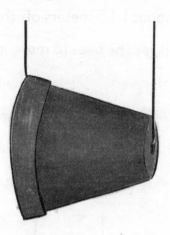

6. Cut the bamboo to fit inside your pot or plastic bottle. Make them a bit shorter than the length of your pot or bottle.
7. Tie the bundle of bamboo together with a piece of string.
8. Place some modelling clay in the bottom

of the pot or bottle and stick the canes into the clay.

9. Hang the bottle horizontally or the pot on its side in your garden in a quiet, secure place, about 1-1.5 meters off the ground, and wait for the bees to move in!

You will know when a bee is staying in your bee hotel because one of the hollow bamboo canes will be filled with a bee nest!

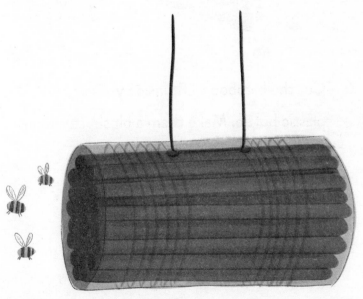

To maintain your bee hotel:

In autumn, move your bee hotel to somewhere dry and unheated like a shed to protect the eggs inside. Move it back outside in spring. After the new bees have emerged in spring or summer (the bamboo holes will be open again) you can replace the bamboo canes.

Look out for more of Tilly's adventures in her next books!

TIGER IN TROUBLE

POLAR BEAR PATROL

THE ORPHAN ORANGUTAN

JESS BUTTERWORTH

Jess was born in London and spent her childhood between the UK and India. She studied creative writing at Bath Spa University and is the author of many books for children. She's filled *The Adventure Club* series with all the things she loved as a child (and still loves to this day!).